MIRACLE
ON 34TH STREET

Adapted by Francine Hughes
Based on the 1947 Motion Picture Screenplay by
George Seaton and Story by Valentine Davies
Screenplay by George Seaton and John Hughes

SCHOLASTIC INC.
New York Toronto London Auckland Sydney

TWENTIETH CENTURY FOX PRESENTS A JOHN HUGHES PRODUCTION A LES MAYFIELD FILM "MIRACLE ON 34TH STREET" RICHARD ATTENBOROUGH ELIZABETH PERKINS DYLAN McDERMOTT J.T. WALSH
JAMES REMAR WITH MARA WILSON AND ROBERT PROSKY MUSIC BY BRUCE BROUGHTON COSTUMES DESIGNED BY KATHY O'REAR EDITED BY RAJA GOSNELL PRODUCTION DESIGNER DOUG KRANER DIRECTOR OF PHOTOGRAPHY JULIO MACAT EXECUTIVE PRODUCERS WILLIAM RYAN AND WILLIAM S. BEASLEY
BASED ON THE 1947 MOTION PICTURE TO BE SCREENPLAY BY GEORGE SEATON AND STORY VALENTINE DAVIES SCREENPLAY BY GEORGE SEATON AND JOHN HUGHES PRODUCED BY JOHN HUGHES DIRECTED BY LES MAYFIELD ©1994 TWENTIETH CENTURY FOX

ISBN 0-590-22507-3

12 11 10 9 8 7 6 5 4 3 2 1   4 5 6 7 8 9/9
Designed by Madalina Stefan

Printed in the U.S.A.   24
First Scholastic printing, December 1994

It was Thanksgiving morning in New York City. Already people were lining the streets, getting ready to watch the Cole's Thanksgiving Day Parade. They couldn't wait to see the marching bands, grand floats, colorful balloons, and—best of all—a real, live Santa Claus riding in an elegant sleigh.

"Santa Claus!" said Dorey Walker, head of Special Projects for Cole's Department Store. She was bustling around the parade site making sure everything was in place, and she'd just realized that the actor she had hired to play Santa Claus was nowhere to be seen!

Dorey was worried about the parade, *and* about Cole's. Located on 34th Street, in the heart of the city, Cole's was the oldest, most beloved store in New York. But a scheming businessman named Victor Lamberg was trying to take it over. He wanted Cole's to be just another big impersonal store in his Shoppers Express chain. Cole's was in trouble.

And so was Dorey, unless she could find another Santa.

Just then Dorey spotted an old gentleman threading his way through the crowd. He had a fluffy white beard, rosy-red cheeks, and a bright warm smile.

"Sir?" said Dorey, stepping in front of him. "Would you please be our Santa Claus?" She cast a professional eye over the gentleman. "You don't even have to change. Just be yourself, and you'll do fine."

Still smiling, the old man introduced himself. His voice was calm and gentle. And it made Dorey feel better just listening to it. "My name is Kriss," he said. "Kriss Kringle."

Did he say Kriss Kringle? Dorey looked at him strangely. She didn't care for make-believe stories about Santa. She was too no-nonsense for that. But she did know that was another name for Santa Claus. Did this man believe he was Santa?

But Dorey didn't have time to ask questions. Kriss was already climbing aboard the sleigh, crying, "Now, Dasher! Now, Dancer! Now, Prancer and Vixen! On Comet! On Cupid! On Donder and Blitzen!"

Slowly, the float rolled down the street. Old people, young people, rich, poor, and everybody in between gazed at Kriss and smiled. For just that moment, when Kriss and his sleigh passed them by, they all believed in Santa.

"It's really Santa Claus!" cried a little girl, as Kriss waved to her. "And he knows me!"

A few blocks away, Dorey's six-year-old daughter was watching the parade from an apartment window.

"You know what, Bryan?" Susan said, turning to face her visiting neighbor. "I know the secret of Christmas. Santa Claus isn't real."

Bryan looked at her, surprised. "Santa Claus not real? Says who?"

"Says my mom," Susan answered, just as Dorey walked inside.

Dorey nodded briskly. She didn't want her daughter believing in silly fantasies. She didn't want her hurt when she found out the truth. After all, Susan didn't have a dad. And it was up to Dorey to be honest with her—no matter what.

The next morning, Cole's Department Store was jammed with people. It was busier than it had been in years. Everybody wanted to see the new Santa Claus—the Santa who seemed so real. A line of children snaked around Santa's Workshop, as one by one Kriss Kringle placed them on his knee.

"Now tell Santa what you'd like for Christmas," Kriss said to each child.

The children poured out their hearts. And Kriss helped each and every one, giving money to needy moms, telling dads where to shop for toys and games—even if it meant sending them to other stores.

"Any store that puts a parent ahead of making money has *my* business," one woman told Dorey. "I'm a Cole's shopper now. Because… " —she paused for a moment, looking thoughtful—"your Santa is the real thing!"

The word spread quickly about Kriss. Giving, generous, he could speak to children in any language, and he always seemed to know them personally… as if he'd been bringing them gifts for years.

Each morning now, a crowd of customers waited outside Cole's for the doors to open. And when they did, the people burst inside, eager to shop, eager to see Santa.

⭐ Business was booming. And Victor Lamberg was angry. "Cole's is making a lot of money," he told his employees. "And the more money they make, the harder it will be for me to take over. I want something done about this...." His mouth was set in a firm, hard line. "Now!"

The days grew colder as Christmas drew closer. One brisk wintry day, Bryan took Susan to Cole's and, gently urging her forward, put her in line to see Santa. Feeling awkward, Susan sat on Kriss's lap.

"You're a very good actor," Susan told him. "Your whiskers look almost real."

"They are real," Kriss said, a twinkle in his eye. "Go ahead and pull."

Susan gave a tug. The whiskers *were* real. Kriss's very own red suit, with its bright brass buttons, seemed real, too. And so did his smile. Was he for real?

Before Susan could decide, Dorey rushed over and whisked her away.

That night, Susan couldn't sleep. Getting out of bed, she padded into the living room where her mother was working.

"Mom," said Susan, "what if Kriss Kringle really *is* Santa?"

Dorey made room for Susan on the couch and hugged her close. "Honey, there is no Santa Claus. But why don't you ask Mr. Kringle for something? Something that you'd never ask me for. And if you don't get it on Christmas morning, then you'll know the truth."

Thinking hard, Susan went back to bed. She knew what she wanted more than anything in the world. But could she really ask for it?

Bright and early the next morning, Dorey went off to work. Walking past Santa's Workshop, she stopped a moment to say, "Good morning," and help Kriss get ready for the flood of customers.

"I know you and your daughter don't believe in me," Kriss told her softly. "But if you can't believe...if you won't believe...then you are doomed to a life of doubt."

Dorey, silent, looked at him questioningly. He seemed so concerned, so sad.

"And what kind of life is that?" he added gently.

All around the city, the magic of Christmas was working its spell. Bryan felt it. Children, grown-ups, even Dorey, felt it. And, one night, when Kriss Kringle was paying a visit, Susan felt it, too—a twinge of hope. A hope there *was* a Santa Claus, after all.

"There has to be something you want for Christmas," Kriss was saying to her as he tucked her into bed. "Something you want very much."

Susan sighed, not sure she should say anything.

"I'm good at keeping secrets," Kriss added.

Finally, Susan showed him a picture of a family, sitting on the porch of a pretty little house.

"That's what I want for Christmas," she told him. " A house and a family."

A house and a family was a tall order. Kriss walked down the street, deep in thought. Suddenly, a voice called out to him. "Hey, goofball!"

Kriss turned around.

"Yeah, I'm talking to you," a man said meanly. "You're just a nutty old man. You're crazy, thinking you're Santa. What do you care about kids anyway?"

The man stepped up to Kriss, pressing his face close to Kriss's. "Kids aren't good for anything! And you know it!" He gave Kriss a push.

Kriss grew angry. It was one thing calling him crazy. But it was quite another, saying that about children. He pushed back.

The man screamed, falling to the ground as a police car roared over and a photographer snapped pictures.

"Stop that man!" a woman cried. "He's the Santa from Cole's. And he attacked this poor man!"

Kriss stood there, shaking and confused. He'd hardly pushed the man at all. The man was only pretending to be hurt. What was going on?

Kriss didn't know that the woman, the nasty man, and the photographer all worked for Victor Lamberg. And this was all part of a plan—a plan to make trouble.

Within hours, the story was on the front page of every newspaper in the city: SANTA CLAUS IS CRAZY! KRISS KRINGLE GOES NUTS! SENT TO HOSPITAL!

Victor Lamberg sat in his office and smiled as he read the headlines. His plan was working well. Soon Cole's would belong to him.

Across the street, Dorey pushed her way past the crowd at Cole's. She had to do something to help! Right at that moment, a judge was deciding if Kriss had to stay in the hospital—permanently.

But, Dorey wondered, is Kriss really crazy? Or is he—

Dorey caught her breath. Santa Claus! All at once, she realized. She did believe in Kriss. She did believe in Santa! She wouldn't live a life of doubt—not anymore!

Quickly, Dorey reached for the phone, ready to dial Bryan's number. Bryan was a lawyer. And Kriss Kringle needed a lawyer. Desperately.

As soon as he hung up the phone with Dorey, Bryan raced to the judge's chambers. Ed Collins, the lawyer arguing against Kriss, was already there, smiling broadly.

Judge Harper was just about to sign the papers stating Kriss was too dangerous to be released from the hospital. His pen hovered above the dotted line.

"Wait!" said Bryan, bursting into the room. "If your honor pleases, I request a formal hearing."

Ed Collins frowned. This wasn't going according to plan. He worked for Victor Lamberg—and Victor Lamberg was paying him to make sure Kriss was sent away.

As soon as Bryan left, Ed Collins turned to Judge Harper. "Mr. Lamberg knows you need money for your re-election campaign. He'll give you that money, if. . ." His voice trailed off.

The judge nodded. He understood. All he had to do was decide that Kriss Kringle was crazy.

But all across New York City, people were deciding for themselves.

They called Cole's Department Store to say, "Yes, we believe!"

They hung signs in windows. They shouted in the streets. "Yes, we believe! We believe!"

They gathered outside Cole's each day to show their support.

The entire city was standing behind Kriss Kringle. The entire city believed. And an entire city waited with bated breath for the hearing to begin.

It was the day before Christmas. Inside a courtroom, Ed Collins called Kriss Kringle to the stand. Kriss walked with his head held high, waving to Dorey and Susan in the audience.

"I hope he turns out to be Santa," Susan whispered to her mom. "Then everything will be okay.

And we'll have a home and family," she added to herself.

"Mr. Kriss Kringle," Ed Collins said loudly. "Do you believe you are Santa Claus?"

Kriss didn't hesitate for a moment. "Yes," he said proudly.

That was all Ed Collins needed to hear. "I rest my case," he told the judge.

Next it was Bryan's turn to present his case. "Your honor," he said, "I should like to call my first witness."

A little girl walked through the courtroom and sat in the witness stand.

"Who gives you Christmas presents?" Bryan asked.

The girl pointed to Kriss. "He does."

"And what's his name?"

"Santa Claus."

"And how can you be sure he's Santa Claus?"

"Because he looks just like him and he's very, very nice."

"Enough!" shouted Ed Collins, rising from his seat. "This is ridiculous. We don't even have proof there is a Santa Claus!"

"Your honor, can Mr. Collins prove there *isn't* one?" Bryan shot back.

Ed Collins acted quickly. He brought in experts who'd been to the North Pole and had never seen Santa's Workshop. He brought in reindeer that couldn't fly. And when Kriss explained the Workshop was invisible, and that reindeer don't fly until Christmas Eve, Ed Collins called Kriss crazy. He said, "Mr. Kringle might hurt a child."

With that, Susan jumped out of her seat. "Hey, you big jerk!" she cried. "Mr. Kringle's the nicest man in the world. He'd never hurt anybody!"

"Order! Order!" roared the judge, banging his gavel. But deep inside, he agreed with Susan. For one long moment, Judge Harper thought about Susan, and the little girl who'd taken the stand. He had a grandson just about her age. Then he thought about the millions of New Yorkers who called in to Cole's, who hung signs, who shouted in the streets, "We believe!"

Of course, there was the money. Judge Harper would lose that if he decided to let Kriss Kringle go free. But somehow, the money didn't seem important anymore.

"It is the will of the people that guides the government," the judge announced. "And I have seen the people's faith in Santa Claus. Accordingly, Santa does exist. And he exists in the person of Kriss Kringle!"

A great cheer swept the courtroom. Kriss was free!

"You made believers out of everyone," Bryan told him. "Even Dorey."

But Kriss knew there was somebody who still wasn't sure about Santa. Someone who wanted a house and a family for Christmas.

Nighttime drew near and the skies turned dark. Under bright stars, carolers roamed the streets, singing. It was Christmas Eve.

Dorey was alone, reading her mail, when she saw the note from Bryan. *Meet me at St. Patrick's Cathedral*, it read. At that same exact moment, Bryan was opening a note of his own, signed by Dorey.

Neither one had sent a note to the other. But when they met, it didn't seem to matter .

Outside, a gentle snow was blanketing the city. And inside the cathedral, Dorey and Bryan reached for each other. It all felt so right…so magical…they knew. They were there to get married.

Christmas morning, Susan jumped out of bed in a flash. Had her Christmas wish come true? She rushed to the tree, hoping for a sign, and saw Dorey and Bryan holding hands.

"You're married!" Susan cried, throwing her arms around them both. "I have a family!"

Then Dorey and Bryan took Susan to a little house—just like the one in the picture. Only this house had *their* names on the mailbox.

"It's a Christmas bonus from Cole's," Dorey explained. But Susan knew the truth.

"Kriss got me everything I asked for," she shouted happily. "He really *is* Santa Claus!"

And somewhere far away, already moving on to another city, to another place where people needed to believe, Kriss Kringle smiled. "Merry Christmas, Susan," he whispered. "Merry Christmas to all."